PUFFIN BOOKS

ONE NIL

Football! Dave Brown is absolutely mad about football. He dreams about it all the time, even when he's supposed to be concentrating on the arithmetic problem on the blackboard . . .

One day Dave discovers that the England squad are coming to train at his local club. He desperately wants to go and see them – but he will be at school. There seems to be no solution for his problem – or is there?

Find out how Dave takes on his mum and beats her, avoids school and scores the goal of a lifetime – and how he is finally beaten at his own game!

A funny and exciting story for young readers, illustrated with lots of line drawings.

Tony Bradman is deputy editor of *Parents* magazine. *One Nil* is his first novel, and – in case you haven't already guessed it – he's mad about football!

TONY BRADMAN

ONE NIL

Illustrated by Jon Riley

PUFFIN BOOKS

For my mum,
who caught me out
more than once

Puffin Books Penguin Books Ltd, Harmondsworth, Middlesex, England
Viking Penguin Inc., 40 West 23rd Street, New York, New York 10010, U.S.A.
Penguin Books Australia Ltd, Ringwood, Victoria, Australia
Penguin Books Canada Limited, 2801 John Street, Markham, Ontario, Canada L3R 1B4
Penguin Books (N.Z.) Ltd, 182–190 Wairau Road, Auckland 10, New Zealand

First published by Viking Kestrel 1985
Published in Puffin Books 1987

Made and printed in Great Britain by
Richard Clay Ltd, Bungay, Suffolk

Typeset in 16/22pt Monophoto Palatino

Chapter One

Football, football, football. Dave Brown was mad about football. In fact, you could say that he was absolutely potty about the game.

Which is why he wasn't listening to Mrs Adams, his teacher, when he should have been. Instead of concentrating on the blackboard and the arithmetic lesson (Dave hated arithmetic, anyway), he was lost in a dream.

In his mind, it was the last minute of extra time in the World Cup Final. The score was nil all, and there was everything to play for – and Dave was playing too. He was playing up front for England, and yes ... he was making a run into the penalty area, and winger Keith Bosley, the winger he'd seen so often on the television, Keith

Bosley was on a speed run down the wing, and now his beautifully struck cross was drifting in over the defenders' heads, Dave was rising to meet it, his head was striking it cleanly and firmly . . . and it was in the back of the net, beyond the beaten keeper! One nil to England, and Dave was the hero! They'd won the World Cup!

'Goal!' shouted Dave. He stood up to fling his arm in the air triumphantly – and knocked his chair over with a clatter.

'David Brown! What on earth do you think you're doing?'

Mrs Adams was staring at Dave as if he was completely round the twist. Mind you, she wasn't the only one giving him a funny look. The whole class was staring at him, and Dave could feel his cheeks slowly beginning to turn a bright, Manchester United red.

'Well, David?' Mrs Adams was beginning to look quite cross. 'We're all waiting for an explanation.' Dave could hear a lot of hushed giggling going on around him now. But he didn't dare look at anyone else. What could he say to Mrs Adams? What was it his Dad always said? 'When in doubt, say sorry.' Dave thought that sounded like very good advice. He swallowed hard.

'I'm er, sorry, er, miss.'

Mrs Adams put her hands on her hips. She still looked cross.

'Sorry isn't really good enough, David Brown.' She paused. 'Just make sure you pay a little more attention in future.'

'Yes, miss.'

'I'm sure we're all very proud of your efforts for the school football team.'

'Yes, miss.'

Mrs Adams wagged her finger at him.

'But there's more to life than playing football, you know.'

'Yes, miss,' said Dave – although he couldn't think of anything that was quite as important as football.

Mrs Adams smiled – at last.

'Besides,' she said, 'if you don't pay attention to what I'm trying to teach you, you'll never be able to keep track of how many goals you score.'

'He never scores any, miss,' said Carla Bates. 'Every time he gets in front of the goal he falls over.' Dave stuck his tongue

out at her. She was always having a go at
him.

'Sounds just like when you're playing
netball,' he said. Carla stuck her tongue out
at him.

'All right, all right, you lot,' said Mrs
Adams. 'Put your tongue away, Carla, it's
far too early in the day to look at
something as nasty and unpleasant as that.
Sit *down*, Jane, and stop pulling Tracey's
hair, Lee . . . let's get on with some work!'
She turned to the blackboard and tapped on
it hard with her piece of chalk, which broke

in half. Mrs Adams tut-tutted. 'Now, where was I?'

Mrs Adams picked up the lesson where she had left off. Dave tried to concentrate and to follow what she was saying, but the effort was too much for him. It wasn't long before he was making that run into the penalty area again and rising to meet Keith Bosley's cross . . .

'David Brown!' It was Mrs Adams's voice, and not the referee's, which broke into Dave's dream once more. 'David Brown, will you *please* pay attention! Or would you like to see the Head?' She looked really cross, this time.

'Er, sorry, miss, no miss, er . . .'

'All right, all right . . . I don't know, David. Football's going to be your downfall one of these days.'

'Yes, miss.'

But Dave didn't really believe it.

Chapter Two

Dave didn't believe what his best friend
Derek Williams told him on the way home
from school that day either.

'You're kidding,' said Dave. 'You must be
joking!'

'It *is* true,' Derek was saying. 'My dad
told me that the full England squad are
going to be training at the City ground on
Friday morning.'

Derek's dad should know, thought Dave.
After all, he was the chief groundsman at
City, their local, lowly fourth division club.
Dave started dribbling a crushed can down
the pavement in front of him. He took it
round two lamp posts, stopped, and shot
for goal. The can bounced off a car with a

clang. A window flew open and a man's head appeared.

'Oi! Clear off!' he shouted. 'And if you've scratched my car, I'll . . .'

Dave and Derek didn't wait to hear what he would do. They ran off down the road, laughing fit to bust. They shot round the corner and burst into the park where they usually stopped for a half hour's kick-about

on the way home from school. Derek was also in the school team with Dave, and they were best mates. Dave had often gone down to the City ground with Derek, who could get in almost any time he wanted because his dad worked there.

But today they didn't have a kick-about. They went over to the swings and sat on a roundabout next to each other. Dave hugged the ball they'd brought with them to his chest.

'My dad says it's all supposed to be very secret,' said Derek as they slowly went round.

'I suppose they want to practise some set-piece moves without anyone seeing them,' said Dave. 'It's the big match next week, isn't it?' England were due to play France in a World Cup qualifier at Wembley.

'My dad says I can have the day off to

come down and watch them train,' said
Derek. 'Do you fancy coming down
too?'

Dave closed his eyes. The roundabout
was still going round and round, and in his
mind's eye he dreamed that he was standing
on the centre spot at Wembley, turning
round and round so that he could wave to
the whole crowd. He couldn't think of
anything that he would rather do in the
world than watch England training – unless
it was to pull on an England shirt, trot out
on to the Wembley pitch and score a goal.
He could see Keith Bosley crossing the ball,
he could hear the crowd roaring . . .

'But your mum won't let you have the
day off school though, will she?' said Derek.

Dave slumped down over the ball in his
arms. Derek was right. He knew that it
wasn't even worth asking his mum if he
could have the day off school. When it
came to taking time off, his mum was a
holy terror. If she even so much as thought
that you were trying to skive off, all hell

was likely to break loose. And as far as football was concerned, Dave's mum agreed with Mrs Adams. She didn't think it was very important at all.

Dave felt really miserable. The England squad — including Keith Bosley — were going to be so close . . . but they might as well go training on the moon for all the good it would do him.

And then he had an idea.

He sat forward, then jumped off the roundabout.

'I'll be there, Derek!' he was shouting. 'I'll be there!'

He *knew* he'd be there, too . . . it was a great idea. Dave was so pleased with himself that he kicked the ball as high as he could.

'Maybe we'll even get picked for the squad,' he laughed as he waited for the ball to spin down out of the sky.

'Maybe we'll even get a game!'

Derek laughed too – and he laughed
even more when the ball landed on Dave's
head when Dave wasn't looking.

Chapter Three

Dave's mum was standing beside the bed.

'Are you sure you don't feel well?'

Dave looked over the blankets at her face. He knew that this was the crucial moment. If he could convince her now, she'd leave him alone, go off to work — and he'd be away, home and dry.

'I feel rough, mum, honest I do.' That had sounded all right; weak, ill, suffering — but not too much. He didn't want her calling out the doctor, or worse, volunteering to stay at home and look after him.

For the whole plan depended on making sure that Dave's mum went to work. His idea had been a very simple one; he was simply going to pretend that he was ill. He had put the plan into operation the night before. After tea he had flaked out on the sofa and said that he had a headache. Then he'd gone to bed early, complaining of a sore throat. He'd even missed his favourite science fiction programme on the television, but it would all be worth it – if the plan worked.

Dave's mum sat down on the side of the bed and put her hand on his forehead. He could feel the cold metal of her rings on his skin.

'You do feel as if you've got a bit of a

temperature,' she said, looking deep into his eyes. Dave tried to keep a straight face. Under the bedclothes he was wearing two vests, his pyjamas, two jumpers *and* his track suit top. He was boiling — but it was all part of the plan.

'There is a lot of flu going round at the moment. Doreen at work's just gone down with it, and so's her Julie,' his mum said. But she still didn't look really convinced.

Dave decided that now was the moment to play his trump card.

'I won't be missing much at school, anyway. It's P.E. all this afternoon,' he said. He tried to sound as weak and wistful as he could. 'Mr Castle will probably send us out on a run.' He paused for effect. 'And it looks as if it's going to rain,' he said, turning his eyes to the grey sky beyond the bedroom window.

His mum's face changed immediately.

Dave knew then that he'd made it. He felt as if he'd just scored the winner at the Cup Final . . . but he had to keep a straight face. The effort was making his toes curl.

'That settles it,' his mum said, standing up. 'You certainly don't want to be out there running about in the cold and wet. You'll get pneumonia.' She stood up, then bent down to kiss him. Dave could feel that she'd left half her lipstick behind on his forehead.

'Now you stay indoors, no running about outside or playing football in the garden,' she said. 'Mrs Jones is still cross about her broken window. You're lucky to have got your ball back, my lad.'

Dave watched his mum walk over to the bedroom door. 'I'll make an appointment for you at the doctor's tonight if you're still not better when I get home.' She stopped with her hand on the door and looked back at Dave. 'I don't like leaving you on your own though . . .' she said. Dave held his breath. What was going on in his mum's mind? Would he make it? Or would it all fall to pieces, now that he was so close to getting what he wanted?

'I'll be all right, mum,' he said.

'I don't know . . .' Then his mum smiled. 'I know what I'll do. I'll get Mrs Grant to pop in and have a look at you a bit later.' Dave's heart sank. 'And your sister will be back from school by half past four, so you'll be all right.'

She blew him a kiss and went out of the door.

Dave heard her going down the stairs. He listened to her stop by the front door to put on her coat. He heard the front door being opened.

'Bye now,' his mum's voice floated up the stairs. 'Just you make sure you behave yourself!'

'I will! Bye!' Dave remembered at the last moment that he still had to sound ill, so his 'bye' came out sounding as if he was being strangled. His mum didn't seem to notice though. She didn't come back upstairs, at any rate.

Dave heard the front door close behind her.

He lay still for a second, listening to her footsteps go up the path, the gate swing open and shut with a dull clang, her footsteps going up the street until they faded completely.

Then he sprang out of bed and began to strip off all those layers of clothes. Another minute and he would have melted! He followed his mum in his mind. By now she'd be going round the corner. She'd stop off at Mrs Grant's, then go into the newsagent to buy a newspaper. Then she'd go and wait at the bus stop. The bus would arrive in a couple of moments,

she'd get on, pay her fare and sit down.
In ten minutes she'd be at the gate of
Bridgehead's, where she worked. In a quarter
of an hour his mum would be at her desk
in the office, safely occupied and out of his
way for the rest of the day.

It would have worked perfectly . . . if
only mum hadn't gone and asked Mrs
Grant to look in later on. Dave stopped in
the middle of taking off one of his jumpers
and sat down on the edge of his bed. He
racked his brain to think of a way round
this new obstacle. But he couldn't risk going
out if Mrs Grant was going to turn up
some time during the morning . . . if she
did, and he wasn't in, she'd have mum home
straight away. Dave's eyes widened as a
horrifying thought popped into his mind. If
Mrs Grant didn't know where he was, she
might even call out the police – and then
he'd be in trouble!

He wasn't going to make it. He was going to miss the England squad, and after he'd got so close ...

Chapter Four

Just at that moment, the phone began to ring. Dave got off his bed and trudged down the stairs feeling very, very gloomy indeed. He picked up the receiver.

'Hello?' he said. He remembered just in time that he was supposed to sound ill. He threw in a few coughs as well, just to make it sound really authentic. After all — it could be anybody on the other end. It might even be his mum, or Mrs Adams checking up on him!

But it wasn't. It was Mrs Grant.

'Hello? David? Is that you?' Dave wondered who else it could be, but he didn't say anything cheeky to Mrs Grant. You weren't supposed to be cheeky when you were ill. 27

Dave could hear Tom, Mrs Grant's baby, crying in the background. In fact, young Tom was crying so hard that Dave could hardly hear what Mrs Grant was saying.

'Yes, it's me.'

'I hear you're not feeling too good,' she said.

'I'm not too bad,' Dave said, as quietly and pathetically as he could manage.

'You'll have to speak up, David,' Mrs Grant said. 'I can't hear a word you're saying with Tom crying like that.'

'I'm not too bad,' Dave said – a lot more loudly.

'Oh, right. Anyway,' Mrs Grant continued over the noise of her baby's howling, 'your mum's asked me to pop in later on to see if you're all right.'

'Yes, she said she was going to ask you.' Dave felt very, very depressed.

'Anyway, David, the thing is that I've got a few things to do, and then I've got to pop out to the shops . . .' her voice was drowned out by a particularly loud scream from Tom.

'I'm sorry?' said Dave.

'Anyway, I don't think I'll be back until at least one o'clock. You'll be OK until after I've given Tom his lunch, won't you? I should be there by half past one, at the latest. Your mum said she'd left you some soup in the fridge I can do for you.'

Dave couldn't believe his ears. He started doing some quick mental arithmetic. He smiled to himself — Mrs Adams would be proud of him! He looked at the hall clock . . . it was just gone nine; Derek had said that the squad would start their training session at about ten. It would probably be over by twelve . . . Dave nearly cried out for joy. He could make it!

'David? David, are you still there?' Mrs Grant's voice and Tom's crying were still in his ear.

'I'm here, Mrs Grant.'

'Will you be all right this morning? I'll pop in earlier if you want me to.'

'No, no . . . I'll be all right,' he said. 'I'll read some books and watch the telly.'

'OK. I'll see you later then.'

'Yes, Mrs Grant.'

Mrs Grant rang off. Dave stood in the
hall, his fists clenched, his eyes closed, and
his mind full of Wembley and scoring
goals and England and the World Cup and
Keith Bosley. He'd made it. One last bit of
luck, and the plan had worked out like a
dream. He could go and see England train
at the City ground. Dave laughed out loud.

'Dave – one, mum – nil!' he said, and
bounded up the stairs to his bedroom.

Chapter Five

Dave chose his clothes carefully. He put
on a tee-shirt, and then his favourite
football shirt — the Spurs one with a
number eight on the back — over that. He
pulled on his football socks, then his jeans,
and tucked the bottoms of the legs into his
socks; finally, he put on his best trainers and
did them up nice and tight.

He picked up his football boots, too, then
went downstairs and into the kitchen. Dave
had never skived off school much. He could
only remember doing it once or twice
before; he was too worried about what his
mum would say if she caught him out to
do it more often. So the quiet of the house
was unusual, almost creepy. Dave could
hear the fridge humming and the hall clock

ticking, and his footsteps sounded really
loud.

He was used to the house being full of
noise, like it had been this morning, with his
dad bellowing for a clean shirt and his mum
telling him where the iron was, and his
sister with a radio on as loud as it would
go. Dave decided he didn't mind it being
quiet; it made a change, anyway.

But if he was to get the best out of today, he had to be out on the road pretty soon. He looked at the clock again — there would be a bus on the corner in five minutes, according to the timetable he'd looked at on his way home last night. And Dave didn't want to miss a second of the training session. He went into the hall, put on his tracksuit top and then his anorak over that, and stepped out of the front door.

He'd nearly closed it behind him when he pulled himself up short. He'd almost forgotten his front door key! The thought of coming back and finding himself locked out made him go all hot and sweaty, despite the rain and the cold wind. With a sigh of relief, he nipped back inside, picked up his key from the hall table next to the phone and stepped out again.

It had been a near thing. But as he shut

the door behind him, the key firmly in his hand, he couldn't help laughing to himself. Today was going to be a dream.

Dave pulled the hood of his anorak tightly around his face — partly to keep the rain out, but also to make sure that none of the neighbours recognized him. He walked quickly along the street, sticking as closely as he could to the hedges and garden walls. He was relieved to see the bus arrive at the corner just as he got there — he wouldn't have to take the risk of standing around waiting.

Mind you, he already had his story all prepared if someone stopped him and asked why he wasn't at school. He was simply going to say that he was late. And on the way back he could say he was going home for lunch! It was really easy!

Dave went upstairs on the bus and sat right at the back, huddled down. He looked out over the wet, empty streets. Everything looked different somehow. They were quiet, deserted, and they looked as if they were waiting to be used again when everybody started coming home from school or from work. There was hardly anyone about, just the occasional old lady or mum pushing a pram to the shops.

And then Dave saw a policeman.

He ducked down as quickly as he could, hoping that he hadn't been seen. That was the trouble about skiving off – it was all a bit nerve-racking. You had to stay clear of

places where you might be seen by someone from school or anyone else who might know you. And if a policeman saw you out while everyone else was at school, he might start asking awkward questions. Dave could feel his heart racing. He thought that this story about being late would probably stand up . . . but he couldn't be sure, could he?

In fact Dave began to think that skiving wasn't a very good idea after all. The last time he'd done it, he'd been so worried about getting caught that he hadn't dared step outside the door. Which meant that he'd ended up hanging around bored at home. It had been worse than having to stay at home when you really were ill.

But he had something to do today, somewhere to go — something to see that you didn't get a chance to see every day of your life. Dave sat up and peeped out of the window. He couldn't see the policeman any more — but he could see that he'd nearly arrived at the City ground. There was the main stand looming against the sky.

The England squad were probably inside it already. And the chance to see them was almost worth getting caught out, even by his mum. Dave jumped up from his seat and swung down the stairs. He sprang off the bus and started running towards the side entrance Derek had told him to use. The players' entrance . . .

'And it's Dave Brown racing up the wing . . .' he began to say to himself as he ran into the ground. What a day it would be!

Chapter Six

At first Dave wondered for a terrible
moment if Derek had been having him on.
The ground looked deserted, and he
couldn't hear a sound. But as he walked
down the touchline he began to hear
shouting in the distance. He looked up, into
the stand opposite, and saw some figures
running up and down the terraces. A voice

floated across the pitch, and an echo went round the ground.

'Put some muscle into it, John . . . it's no good unless it hurts! Get those knees up, Terry . . . up! up! up! Come on, Keith, let's see some effort, some real effort . . .'

They were all there – the full England squad – and it looked as if they were being worked really hard by the assistant coach, Jimmy Taylor. Dave knew that the professionals always started a full training session with some loosening up and some fitness exercises, perhaps even a run. But this looked like torture. Jimmy Taylor had them all running up the steep terraces to the top and back down again – and then straight back up.

Dave walked along the touchline and peered into the stand opposite. It was in shadow, so he couldn't see much, and the sky was darkening with rain clouds, which didn't make it any easier. But he could make out some familiar faces even from that side of the pitch, faces he'd only ever seen on television before. Yes, there he was, there was Keith Bosley . . .

'Come on, Keith, you look as if you've had it!' Jimmy Taylor's voice echoed across the ground. Keith Bosley put on a sprint, but soon slowed down.

'Hey, Dave! You made it then! You escaped!'

Derek was jogging down the touchline towards him.

'Yeah, I'm ill,' he laughed. 'My mum thinks I'm on my last legs!'

Derek laughed too. 'But what will she do if she finds out? Won't she give you a really hard time?'

'She's not going to find out, is she?' said

Dave. 'At least, I hope she doesn't. If she
did I'd be hung, drawn, and quartered and
banned from football for life.'

They started to walk up the touchline.
Dave could see a group of men standing near
the corner of the pitch up at the canal end.
He recognized one face, at least; it was Bill
Mason – the manager of the England team!

Dave couldn't really believe it. He'd seen
Bill Mason on the television and in all the
newspapers, and now there he was,

standing in that group of men, in the flesh, *real*. Dave suddenly realized that the men surrounding him must be journalists. They seemed to be asking lots of questions, and every time Bill Mason said something they scribbled it down furiously in their notebooks. A couple of them were photographers, judging by the cameras they had slung all over them.

Derek's dad was there too. He saw Dave and Derek approaching, and beckoned them over.

'Dave, come and meet Mr Mason. It's my son and his friend, Mr Mason.'

Bill Mason looked down the touchline at Dave and Derek.

'One more question, Bill . . .' a reporter began to say.

'I think I've answered enough questions for now,' he said. Dave and Derek had reached the group of men. Bill Mason was smiling at them.

'Dave, Derek,' Mr Williams was saying, 'meet Bill Mason, manager of the next World Champions.'

Bill Mason laughed.

'Nice of you to think so,' he said. 'We'll do our best, anyway.' He turned to the two boys and held out his hand. Derek shook hands first, and then it was Dave's turn to experience the England manager's firm handshake. Dave was shaking Bill Mason's hand! It was all a dream, it must be, he thought. He couldn't believe any of it was real.

Chapter Seven

'You a footballer, son?' Bill Mason was talking directly to him, asking him a question.

'Er, yes, sir, I mean, I play for the school team, Mr Mason, er, sir.' Dave could feel everyone's eyes on him and his cheeks burning red.

'Football's the greatest sport in the world,' Mr Mason was saying. 'Do you want to be a professional one day?'

Dave grinned. 'Not half, sir.'

'Keep at it, then, son. Keep at it.' Mr Mason turned to look at his players who were making their way from the stand and on to the pitch. Then he turned back to Dave and smiled again.

'Did the school give you the day off to come down and watch? Pick up a few ideas for the school team, perhaps?'

Dave could feel himself blushing even more deeply.

'Er, well, er, yes, but er, well . . . not exactly . . .' He didn't know what to say, really. But his mouth was open and he had to say something, even if it did all come out sounding like rubbish.

Bill Mason's smile vanished. He started

to wag his finger very slowly at Dave. 'Naughty, naughty . . . you haven't skived off from school, have you?'

'Er, well . . .'

'I'll give you a piece of advice, son, and if I were you, it's advice I'd heed. Football's a tough game. What happens if you don't make it as a professional? Amateur teams are full of good players who weren't good enough to make it in the league. If *you* don't, you'll need something to fall back on, won't you?'

'Yes, sir, I mean, Mr Mason.'

'That's right. You'll need some exam qualifications, a trade. You keep up your school work. It's hard enough getting a job of any sort these days.'

Dave felt that he was blushing from the roots of his hair to the ends of his toes. He didn't know where to look, where to put himself. Everyone seemed to be looking at him – and at Derek, too – so sternly. He thought that Mr Mason would get on very well with his mum – and with Mrs Adams! They all seemed to agree as far as football was concerned, anyway.

But then Bill Mason laughed and ruffled his hair.

'Don't take it to heart, though, son. One day won't make that much of a difference, so long as it is only one day, mind . . . and so long as you promise me that you'll make a special effort in your school work from now on.'

'Oh I will, Mr Mason, I will.'

Bill Mason turned to the journalists. 'I used to have the odd day off myself to go and watch Newcastle United train when I was a lad. My mum nearly killed me when she found out though. She still thinks I should have concentrated on my school work and forgotten about football!' Everyone laughed.

'And if we lose the match next week then I think a lot of people might start to agree with her!' The journalists, Mr Williams, Dave and Derek, all of them laughed again.

'Well, this won't do,' said Mr Mason. 'I'd better make sure the lads are working!' He turned to Dave and Derek again. 'Enjoy your day, boys – and you remember what I've said!' Mr Mason walked on to the pitch, towards the England players.

And Dave did enjoy his day, every second of it. Derek had brought a ball along, and while the squad was finishing off its fitness training and exercises, he and Dave had a kick-about round one of the small, portable training goals the City team used in their training sessions.

But their eyes kept drifting towards the stars out on the pitch. Eventually they saw that the squad was going to practise some set-piece moves, and they ran round behind one of the goals to watch.

Peter Sharpe, one of the two England goalies, was going to be in goal to stop shots. The squad was obviously going to try out some free-kick moves first. Dave and Derek stood a few yards to one side of the goal, watching Peter Sharpe come up to leave his little bag with spare gloves in the back, under a fold of net.

'Hey up, lads, I wouldn't stand there

when that Keith Bosley's shooting. You'd be safer standing in the middle of the goal.'

Dave and Derek laughed, and they laughed even more when they heard the name Keith Bosley called Peter Sharpe. For Dave it was almost like paradise. These were his heroes, and here they were, actually talking and joking with him!

It was great watching the free-kick moves too, promising Peter Sharpe and the other players that they wouldn't breathe a word about their special plans to the French before the big game. Dave almost felt part of the England squad, almost as if he belonged; and he spent most of the morning wrapped in his favourite fantasy, that of pulling on an England shirt and going out to play in the World Cup Final.

He could almost feel the ball at his feet, feel the power surge through his leg as he volleyed the winning goal into the net from

thirty-five yards, feel himself punching the
sky and turning to the acclaim of his team
mates and the wild celebrations of the
crowd . . .

Chapter Eight

'Hey, you two! Wanna game?'

Dave looked at Derek; Derek looked at Dave. Then they both looked towards Keith Bosley, who was running towards them from the little knot of players in the middle of the pitch. He came running up to them, and bent over, resting his hands on his legs just above the knees.

'Well, do you want a game or not? We're
two short for a full side. Bill and Jimmy are
playing for the opposition, so we need a
couple of nifty players.' He was smiling.

Dave looked at Derek; Derek looked at
Dave.

'Yeah!'

And they were on the pitch, trotting
towards the centre spot, towards Dave's
favourite dream. Bill Mason smiled at them
both, then looked around at his assembled
players.

'Well you lot, these two are my secret
weapon. They're a couple of young players
I've been bringing along in secret, and
they're going to give you hell. Remember,
they're after your places.' He winked at
Dave and Derek, a huge, unmissable wink.
Dave couldn't believe it but it was
happening, it really was.

Keith Bosley put him in midfield, on the

right-hand side, and Derek on the left. He laughed and joked with the boys and told them there was no way they could possibly lose today with Sharpey in goal . . . And they were kicking off.

He, Dave Brown, of 41 Sirdar Road, was playing in a training match with the England squad, and playing on the same team as his hero, Keith Bosley. It was a dream come true.

It was all like a dream while he was playing, too, a beautiful dream. Everything he did went right. He passed well, ran off the ball well, even tackled well; although he knew that none of the squad were trying too hard. There was lots of laughing and joking; Danny Thomson, the Aston Villa midfield man, went flying every time he was on the ball and Dave went near him.

'Ref! Ref! That kid's a killer! He's after me all the time!'

The ref was, of course, Bill Mason, who was also playing up front for the opposition. He seemed to be having a lot of fun, even though he was panting a bit. And what made it all the better for Dave was that every time he went near him, Bill Mason shouted some advice.

'Easy, easy now son, look up, head up, look for a spare man, now! That's it, go for the through ball!'

And when the pass was good, Bill Mason would run past and ruffle his hair.

Derek wasn't having a bad game, either.

They were only playing 15 minutes each way, and after they'd changed ends, Dave had the feeling he always had when he was in a match he was enjoying; he didn't want it to end. He would have been happy to play on for days, weeks, months; it was perfect. He dreaded the sound of the final whistle.

He knew it couldn't be far away when he picked up the ball from Keith Bosley just inside the opposition half. Danny Thomson laid back from him, and he could hear other members of the team calling for the ball in space. Derek was to his left, moving towards the area, so he let him have it. Derek put it straight on to Keith Bosley who took it on a speed run to the corner flag, just like in Dave's favourite fantasy!

Dave was moving into the area, calling for the ball. Danny Thomson, a smile still on his face – but with an eye for the ball, just like the professional he was – drifted in with him. Keith Bosley checked his run near the corner flag, beat his marker, and looked up to see where everyone was in the penalty area.

Dave had his arm up, and he was calling for the ball. He looked at Peter Sharpe, who was on his goal line; the goalkeeper smiled

at him, and then looked out at Keith Bosley.
Dave saw the England winger hit the cross
over, and then his eyes were on the ball in
the air. Dave watched it curve over the
heads of everyone in the area. It was
coming towards him, he knew it was
coming directly towards him . . .

And then he was running, his eyes fixed
firmly on that ball. Everything seemed to
have gone into silent slow motion, and
there was nothing else in the world but
Dave and that ball. He was running faster
and faster, he felt both feet leave the
ground, he felt, rather than saw, where the
ball was . . . his forehead connected with its
leather and he sprawled in the goalmouth
mud, sliding to a stop against Peter Sharpe.
The world clicked back into being normal
again; Dave heard voices, shouts, cheering.

He looked up and the net was still
rippling from where the ball had slid down

it and into the back of the goal. He'd
scored with a beautiful diving header.

He'd scored a goal against the England keeper.

One nil!

Chapter Nine

'Great goal, son, great goal!'

It was Keith Bosley who helped Dave up off the ground and patted him so hard on the back that he nearly fell over again.

'You doing anything next Wednesday night? We need a striker.' Keith Bosley had his arm round Dave's shoulders as they walked back to the centre spot. All the other players called out and clapped, and Bill Mason got his whistle out to blow three long, loud blasts – the end of the game.

'Good goal, son, good goal,' he said to Dave. 'Right, that's it, lads.' He turned and shouted at Peter Sharpe. 'And where were you, Sharpey? Eh? Good goal, but you should have taken out the cross!'

'It was too good for him,' shouted Keith Bosley.

'It wasn't the cross, boss — that was rubbish. Any chance of dropping Bosley and playing the lad instead?' Everyone laughed and whistled.

'If I'm out, you're out,' shouted Keith Bosley — and chased Peter Sharpe down the players' tunnel.

Dave heard all this, but he wasn't really listening. He was still stuck in an action replay of his goal. He felt as if he was walking about ten feet above the ground, and the feeling didn't start to fade until he saw some of the players emerging from the dressing room a while later to get in their cars and drive off. Bill Mason had said he could have the ball he'd scored with as a souvenir, and they'd even washed it off and dried it for him so that the squad could

autograph it. They'd done the same for
Derek with another ball.

All the players had a word for him as
they signed the ball, and both Dave and
Derek wished them luck for the match on
Wednesday. One by one the cars started to
disappear from the car park, until there was
only Bill Mason and a couple of the
journalists left . . .

'Can you sign it for me too, Mr Mason?'

'Sure, son.' He pulled out an expensive looking pen and found an empty space on the ball. 'Now you remember what I said about your school work.' He handed the ball back to Dave. 'Why don't you come down to one of City's trials in a couple of seasons? They've got a good apprentice scheme. Could do worse.'

And then he got in his car and drove away.

'Hey Derek, it's been a great day,' said Dave.

'Too right. You've done yourself some favours there, Dave. You'll be playing for England next.'

'You didn't play too badly yourself, Del.'

Dave coughed, and coughed again. He hadn't noticed it up to now, but his throat was beginning to feel a little tickly; he even felt a bit hot and woozy. But he didn't take much notice. He liked what Derek had said, although he couldn't admit to his secret hope — the hope that Bill Mason would remember him.

'Yeah, well, see you.'

'See you.'

Dave sat upstairs on the bus home, looking out at the empty streets. It was just after twelve o'clock and it would only be a few hours before the streets would start filling up again with kids coming home from school, and people knocking off from early shifts. All they'd had was a really boring day, the same as any other. But he had something to remember. The only pity was that it was over, though he'd definitely find out about the City trials.

The only other problem was that he couldn't talk about it either, at least not to his mum or dad. Dad would be really interested, over the moon probably, if he knew; but they'd murder him if they found out he'd been skiving. And that meant he had to hide the signed ball, as well, at least until he could think of a good excuse for having it. Maybe he could say Derek's dad had got it for him. That was it: perfect!

Chapter Ten

Dave let himself into the quiet, empty
house. He made some toast and had a glass
of milk, then realized that his throat felt
more than a bit tickly; it felt sore and he
was coughing a lot now. He was also
beginning to feel hotter, and even shivery
from time to time.

He went upstairs, undressed, stuffed his
mud-spattered clothes in a carrier and
shoved them as far back under the bed as
he could, along with the autographed ball,
and got into bed. He lay caught in an
action replay of his goal for a while,
savouring the perfection of it, the way the
curving flight of the ball had seemed
destined to meet his head as he leaped

towards it, the way the net billowed and rippled as the ball spun down it . . . and he fell asleep with a huge smile on his face. He coughed, too.

Dave didn't remember much more of the afternoon. He didn't remember Mrs Grant coming in to see him, or his sister coming home. He didn't remember his mum coming in and putting her hand on his forehead again, although the coolness of her rings was momentarily pleasant. He didn't remember her clucking over him, and he didn't know that she phoned the doctor, who promised to come in the morning.

He woke briefly, later in the evening, and knew that he was really ill. But it didn't seem to matter. He knew he'd done something very good, but he couldn't remember what it was. Then he fell asleep again.

When he woke the next morning, he felt better, although his throat was still sore and he coughed painfully from time to time. But it didn't seem to matter; he could remember the day before, and just the thought of his goal made him smile. He could hear the noise from downstairs in the kitchen, so everybody else was up and about. He knew that he wouldn't be able to go to school today. He smiled; it wasn't a skive, either, this time.

Just as he was drifting off into an action replay of his goal again, his bedroom door

opened. His sister poked her head round;
she was laughing.

'Who's for the high jump, then?'

Keith Bosley

'What?' he managed to croak, but it was
too late. She was gone. Then he heard
footsteps coming up the stairs and along
the landing towards his door.

It opened, and his mum came in, holding the newspaper.

'How's our invalid this morning?'

Dave tried a weak smile; mum was looking a bit grim.

'I think I feel a bit better.'

'I'm glad, I'm glad.' She was smiling now, but it wasn't a real smile. It looked nasty; Dave had seen it before. It usually came just before a grade A, number one, total telling off. 'I thought you might like to read the paper. I've brought it up for you.'

His mum tossed it at him. Dave looked at her, confused.

'Open it, then. The sports pages.'

Dave opened it. And swallowed hard, even though it hurt his throat. There, right in front of his eyes, in the paper for all to see, was a picture of *him* standing next to Bill Mason. One of those photographers

must have taken it yesterday! There was a headline underneath it, too: 'Mason builds for the future.' There was also a little story about how 'two schoolboys' had been watching England train at City's ground, and one of them had put a goal past Peter Sharpe in a training match. The journalist had written at the end of the story: '. . . and let's hope Sharpey was only kidding about when he got beaten by a kid.'

Dave looked at his mum. It was a killer, really. At any other time he would have been sky-high with pride; not only had he played with the England squad, he'd scored a goal – and got his picture in the paper! But all that was going to happen now was that he was going to get a right roasting from his mum. He tried to shrink back into the bedclothes; he opened his mouth to speak. Mum held up her hand.

'Don't bother. I only hope for your sake that they'll be lenient at school when they see this – and they will.'

Dave hadn't thought of that. He was in trouble. Deep trouble. Mrs Adams would skin him alive when she found out. His heart sank even further.

'Me and your dad were furious. You are never to lie to me like that again. We're the ones who get taken to court if you skive off, you know. If you ever do it again, even once more, I'll . . . I'll . . .'

'Yes, mum.'

Dave's mum sat on the bed. She looked down, and for a moment, he thought she was going to cry. But she looked up and shook her head; then smiled.

'You little . . . I don't know. You should have heard your dad.'

Dave had a feeling he was going to get away with it.

'Was he angry?'

His mum laughed again.

'Angry? He didn't know where to put himself for pride. But he'll still give you a clip round the ear when you're well enough.'

'So you believe I'm ill today?'

His mum cocked her head to one side and looked at him hard.

'I believe you. Thousands wouldn't.'

Dave smiled back at her. But her face changed as she stood up and went to the door.

'But no playing football outside school for a month.'

'But mum!'

It was too late. The door was shut behind her. He heard her voice float up the stairs.

'Mum – one, son – nil.'